Written by Gaby Goldsack
Illustrated by Steve Smallman

This edition published by Parragon in 2009

Parragon
Queen Street House
4 Queen Street
Bath BA1 1HE, UK

ISBN 978-1-4054-1503-3
Printed in China

Tickly Sheep

Illustrated by Steve Smallman

Bath New York Singapore Hong Kong Cologne Delhi Melbourne

One morning, Farmer Fred was in the kitchen having his hair cut. Farmer Fred's wife, Jenny, was snipping away with the scissors.

"Hurry up," said Farmer Fred. "I've got to shear all the sheep today."

"Well, stop wriggling," laughed Jenny.

"But it tickles," chuckled Farmer Fred.

"I've never known anyone make such a fuss about having their hair cut," laughed Jenny, making the final snip.

Farmer Fred and Patch went up to Fern Hill to round up the sheep.

Farmer Fred whistled a signal to Patch: *Peep! Peeeep!* Patch ran around the field, herding the sheep towards the yard.

Farmer Fred whistled a different signal: *Peeeep! Peep!* Patch soon had the sheep lined up outside the barn.

Inside the barn, Farmer Fred switched on his shears. *Whizz, whizz, whizz* went the shears.

"There's nothing quite like shearing sheep," he smiled, and began to sing.

One by one, Farmer Fred sheared
the sheep. The woolly fleeces which
came off the sheep collected on the
barn floor. All went well until it was
Shirley Sheep's turn.

Whizz, *whizz*, went the shears.

"Baa-haa-haa," giggled Shirley Sheep. As soon as the buzzing shears touched her side, Shirley began to wriggle and jiggle. Farmer Fred had forgotten just how ticklish Shirley was!

"Baa-haa-haa," giggled Shirley helplessly.

"Stop wriggling," cried Farmer Fred, as he tried to hold her still.

They made such a noise that all the other animals came to see what was going on.

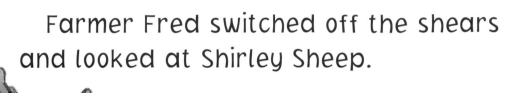

Farmer Fred switched off the shears and looked at Shirley Sheep.

"Rumbling radishes!" he gasped. Shirley had wriggled about so much that she had big bald patches all over her woolly fleece. She looked very peculiar!

"Never fear, I've an idea!" cried Farmer Fred cheerfully.

Farmer Fred dashed off to his workshop with Patch and disappeared inside. The animals gathered around Shirley Sheep. Connie Cow rubbed poor Shirley's head with her nose.

"What's Farmer Fred up to now?" Connie mooed.

"Baaaa!" wailed Shirley Sheep.

Baaaa!

Very soon, Farmer Fred came out of the workshop holding two old tyres tied onto some rope.

"This," Farmer Fred said grandly, "is my Super Sheep-defleecer!"

Farmer Fred helped Shirley Sheep to step through the tyres and slowly lifted her off the ground. Farmer Fred turned on the shears and tried again. And although Shirley wriggled and giggled, Farmer Fred sheared off all her wool.

Farmer Fred let Shirley Sheep down and helped her from the tyres.

"Walloping woolsacks!" said Farmer Fred, looking at Shirley's new woolly coat.

"Baa?" asked Shirley Sheep.
She looked at the other animals.
But they were all laughing so
much they couldn't answer.

While Fred collected up the sheep fleeces, the animals gathered around Shirley Sheep.

"She can't possibly go around looking like that," said Hetty Hen. "Everyone will laugh at her."

"We have to do something," agreed Harry Horse. "Patch, what can we do?"

Suddenly Patch remembered Farmer Fred having his hair cut.

"Woof, woof!" he barked. "Leave it to me."

Patch raced to the kitchen where Jenny had put the scissors, comb and mirror into a bowl.

"Woof, woof!" barked Patch, pushing the bowl outside just as Farmer Fred was crossing the yard.

"What's that Patch?" laughed Fred.
"I haven't got time to give you a hair cut
now." Just then Shirley trotted up.

"Hold on!" said Farmer Fred. "I've had
an even better idea!" He picked up the
bowl and raced back to the barn.

Before long Shirley was sitting in her very own wool-cutting parlour.

"Now, would madam like a short and curly cut?" laughed Farmer Fred, as he began snipping away.

And this time, Shirley didn't giggle or wriggle until all that was left was a curly fringe.

"Perfect," said Farmer Fred, as he tied a huge blue ribbon in Shirley's lovely curls.

Shirley walked proudly around the farmyard. Everyone, including Jenny, gathered around to admire her.

They all agreed that she was the
prettiest sheep on the farm.

"I've never known anyone make such
a fuss about having their hair cut," said
Farmer Fred. Jenny looked at Patch
and laughed.